LUGAR SECRETO

LUGAR SECRETO

Poems and Short Stories

By Chad Fox

For Anita

This is not a book of spells
It's not a book of holy measure
This is a book of passage
And every word
Is an acre of eternity.

Beyond this page is a soft archaic hum.

THE CONTENTS

ONE KEY

key

1 [kee] noun, plural keys, adjective, verb

1. an instrument used in opening such devices as the heart
2. something that affords a means of access: the key to happiness
3. mood or characteristic style, as of expression or thought
4. something that secures or controls entrance to a place
5. keys, spiritual authority –adjective

Origin:

bef. 900; ME key(e), kay(e), OE cǣg, cǣge; c. OFris kei, kai

Synonyms:

answer, explanation, resolution, clue

Page of Hurt

Skeletons keep secrets

In a nest with mating birds

TWO LOVERS

Many ages ago... the sun passed over into the first house of heaven. In this ancient time the planets towered over the earth like large circular monuments and were venerated as the first celestial gods. These planets turned the heavens into a sidereal stage, where great destructive battles unfolded like the collapsing calyx of a rose.

However, suddenly on a quiet night when the Ram was resting in the comfort of the golden wedding garment, the sky lost two of its brightest stars. The outer universe at this time went almost unnoticed due to the luminaries of the sacred planet gods.

These opaque stars shined down in great numbers, warming up the sky like tiny flowers in an endless light bearing garden. It wasn't very often that they caught an observer's eye. The creatures of the earth were too obedient to the five heavenly emperors to take notice of this type of insignificant event. The dust of the two falling stars scattered across the sky like tiny speckles of light and soaked deep into the background of the firmament.

At that moment while skygazing in the forest, a young Rabbit admired the spectacle that had performed so magically above him. His eyes closely examined the place where the two stars had been and the negative space they left behind and was star-struck by its new form. The space had transformed before his eyes from a dense cloudy cluster into the crisp starry image of two lovers. The glow of their new found love traveled down through the Milky Way like a riverbed of soft flowing light.

Dazed and exhausted by the events that unfolded, the Rabbit leaned against a tree, and as the wind played the leaves on the branches above him like an old oak instrument, he carved a heart into the tender surface of the tree's trunk.

The Rabbit had become the shepherd of the forest sky. He sat beneath the tree looking up at the two lovers shining down onto him like a warm blanket of compassion and solvent twilight, which soothed his soul and hunger for life like the warm nourishing milk of a mother.

The soft whisper of the wind and gentle movement of the leaves brushed against his ears, giving to him the humble feeling of rejoice and discovery.

He muttered to himself, just before he fell from his high place of observation, to the lower spheres of sleep and silence, "We are the keepers of beautiful secrets."

The rarest moon.

The Opening

The sky makes a whimper

A squeeze and a nudge

With ladders that take us

To somewhere above

Smile and call her

She holds the key

Her hands are the entrance

That leads her to me.

The Number

Her hearts a music box

It's pretty when it plays

Add a smile to the song

And love is softly made

Her spirit is the kind of light

That over-shines the sun

Absolutely perfect

Like the number after one.

Halo

I grew up in heaven

In the holy land

In between the planets

And the holy lamb

She gave me a comet

I gave her my hand

When we touched each other

It left halos in the sand.

What is this silence that controls the hair on the back of my neck like an impolite puppeteer? What hand moves hearts into curious positions of love and imagination and waits mysteriously behind a large curtain for someone to applaud? Whoever this quiet conductor may be:

Thank you for at least trying.

Broken

Never break a word

They have precious parts

Arranging what is love

To fit a sacred heart

If you want my love

This is where the loving starts

When it ends I hope you know

That it was never hard.

Patriarchs

If I could make these words appear as timeless as the hills and valleys of your *grace*, they would fall into mortal antiquity and written in these lost works it would say,

They fell in love today.

The Boy

The boy is a fish

Alone in the lake

He holds his breath

For as long as it takes.

The Girl

The girl is glowing

Her petals are prim

Like a flower carved

In heaven's hand.

Slow Dance

Awaken lovers
With miracle names
Dance with the angels
With stars on their wings

Wild breath
Heartbeat that we share
Move across the sky
And through our burning hair

Sleeping lovers
Place petals on their bed
Give pleasure to each other
Even after they are dead.

Pillow Boats

Laying down to rest

The pillow boats collide

Eyelids closing down

When it's time to come inside

The lily pads are sleeping

Where the tulips like to hide

When I close my eyes

You're my favorite surprise.

Lover's Crown

Take my hand in love

Wear a golden gown

Tell the sky that you were born

To wear your lover's crown.

The Way

I would hold your hand

Not afraid to lead the way

You would find the moon

And know exactly what to say

We would watch the night

As it fought against the day

We could be the only ones

That loved and got away.

Insect Songs

They evaporate

Like rain drops

They become casual

With love

They make music

Out of insect wings

They must be in heaven.

Breath

Dress her skin with love

In fabric of the night

Look into her golden eyes

And blow away the light.

We touch each other

Like swans when we sleep

THREE SONGS

A celebration is being held in the forest. All creatures of this blessed realm are invited to attend. Before the celebration we will be holding the annual ceremony for: *The New Forest Sun.*

We will march with ribbons into the center alignment and dip the silver pitcher into our lake of lilies, bringing from it waters transfixed by worldly reflection.

The new sun will ascend across the water like a burning chariot pulled by four immortal horses into the water wombs of creation.

The forest sky as we know it today has endured many cataclysmic misadventures that have forced the creatures into a secret way of living, causing them to fall deep into the deluge of an overwhelming shadow.

Many of our higher realm animals have already started to feel the effects the sadness has had on the lower provinces and are aware of its design and deceptive purpose.

The new light predicted by the Old Rabbit will drown this noxious shadow with impressive virtue that will touch the lower valleys of this royal society with its warm and refreshing embrace.

The trees of this old forest will stand tall on this glorious day of celebration, their collective consciousness and wise old voices giving the creatures the benefit of the secret alphabet and the sacred moving vowels of the ancestors.

The world may have forgotten about our old system of love and individuality, but here in our triangle of songs, love and laughter, we have the gift of companionship, and that alone is our enchantment.

Our celebration is one of life and renewal: all creatures will rise a degree in the forest chart, coming closer to our forest architects than we have ever imagined. Prepare yourself for this great day of alignment and restoration.

Instructions:

When midnight comes, follow the cloven path to the old corner stone. There, a card and colored ribbon will be given to you with the name of your light-worker. We will sit beneath the world tree and read these luminous names aloud. When all creatures have connected with their star-guides, we will begin the ceremony.

Be sure to wear your ceremonial attire. Our mother Owl has spent a year of winters sewing fabric together just for this celebration and has blessed us with her heavenly work. The threads are made of golden stems, plucked from the morning light, and the colors are a pallet of potions inspired by the rarest flowers of our fruitful forest.

Daffodil

(Verse 1)

I am the king

Of the daffodil

My heart be still

There's no iris in this field

There's no mercy here

In the silence of the air

There's nothing left but hope

And its hope that got us here.

Daffodil

(Verse 2)

It's all surreal

I wonder what is real

Her eyes reveal

Hidden symbols of the hill

There's no darkness here

Only heavens in her hair

There's nothing left but smoke

In the Serpent's evil lair.

Daffodil

(Verse 3)

We have become

The red that's in the rum

And if the sparrows lie

Then we'll kill them one by one

Save them from the sun

Save them from their selves

And if they ask for mercy, well

Then we shall give them hell.

Daffodil

(Chorus)

We wept through the night

We slept through the sun

We search for the key

But there's only one

We wept through the night

We slept through the sun

We searched for the key

But there's only one.

I'll Give You Love

(Verse1)

Take my heart
I'll give you love
Break my heart
Just make it good

(Chorus 1)

On his head
The crown was dead
The cross was white
The rose was red.

I'll Give You Love

(Verse 2)

Take my name
I'll give you pain
So hell and heaven
Look the same

(Chorus 2)

On his head
The crown was dead
The cross was white
The rose was red.

The Shepherd

(Verse 1)

I keep my eyes in love
My heart is always ready
The symbols of my blood
Keep my bible heavy

(Chorus 1)

Occasional break down
Dreaming of deprivation
Everyone is leaving now
Sacrificial separation.

The Shepherd

(Verse 2)

I sing myself to sleep
My dreams are almost living
The shepherd and the sheep
The king is not forgiving

(Chorus 2)

Occasional breakdown
Dreaming of dispensation
Everyone is singing now
Sacrificial admiration.

If I could write a song that could refine a
single moment, that could keep the
sounds of beauty and love so humbly
confined, I would savor in that miraculous
second, a gentle kiss of the ages; a heart-
song.

FOUR ANIMALS

When Morning Comes

When will morning come

Hurried with its flight

Its wings are tipped with dented gold

That wrap through strands of light

Outside the air is calm

There's a windmill and a dove

Inside we lay in bed all day

Like animals in love.

Sometimes I feel like a lamb

Laying dead on your doorstep

The Sparrow

There the sparrow sits

There the sparrow flies

And somewhere in between

Is where the sparrow dies

Sitting on a branch

Waiting for the sun to rise

So it can tell the other birds

To cross the other side.

The Crane

My tears are golden

They're shaped like the rain

I keep them like pennies

To pay for the pain

I feed the extra

Bread to the crane

When she feels like heaven

Then I feel the same.

Secret Bird

My skeleton is sleeping
Covered up with blood
Inside I'm a funeral
Marching through a flood
Hold my hand forever
Forever we are love
You've become the secret bird
That circles me above.

The Winter Owl

She bathes in the crisp chill of the winter, perched on her throne of ice and tangled evergreen. The clouds pass by like merchant boats, sailing through blue blocks of ice. Her eyes are soft and shimmer like shiny beads of oil. The outside of her breasts are soaked in faded feathers that lay around her body like a thousand drowsy arms.

The moonlight shows a glimpse of her nocturnal self, meant only for the eyes of her creator. Her crest is crowned with forest jewels that vibrate with primitive magic. Her brow sits high, like the peak of an old mountain that was born right here in the bosom of these ancient riverbeds.

She is the knowledge and wisdom of this secret place. Her heart holds within it the sacred initiations of the forest. The winter will eventually end, and she will travel to the top of the holy mountain to take refuge.

The light of the moon will give power to her jewels and place silver stars on the tips of her wings. She will sit gracefully, watching the forest as one of the great guardian watchers of time.

We are the last sacred creatures of this royal forest. It is our spirits that now illuminate the stepping stones, pushing the light into the fine cracks of eternity. Soon the leaves will turn green and become new again, and they will supply enough life to completely cover the canopy of dead branches with the flowers of nature's regeneration.

At this time the Winter Owl will give birth inside a nest of bundled straw and carefully collected rubies. She will sit lovingly upon an orphic egg, entwined by the fire of the forest serpent. She will return from the seven spheres of consciousness with a message to the creatures:

"The sadness cannot last forever and all lovers are a sign of hope and salvation. The time will soon come when nothing but love exists in the forest. Every creature will know this to be true and will find comfort in these woods for years to come."

And so it is told that in this place of secrets, the Lion will forever rule as the divine prince of the day, and the Winter Owl will as always be the queen of our mysterious heaven.

FIVE FLOWERS

Posies

Sleep with lavender

Hold my tired hand

Bend our bones together

So we dream of something grand

Keep the posies dry

And we'll burn them in the sand

We make love in heaven

Like the angels do on land.

Tulips

Crown her with tulips

Jewels and a feather

Find a honey comb

To hold it all together

I speak ancient words

Cause ancient words are better

I would give you all I have

And it would last forever.

Hello little flower
Welcome to my home
I took you from the garden
So I wouldn't dream alone.

The Light Inside

We are not ghosts

Along for the ride

We make the bed

And we sleep on our side

The flowers make us well

They keep our hopes alive

We open up our hearts

To let the light inside.

Pick Me

I am like a flower
Pick me from the ground
Put me in a vase of water
Just don't let me drown
I would give you smiles
Every time you had a frown
We would climb to heaven
On a vine and shimmy down.

Bridge

We have built a bridge

Across a lion's chest

The blood inside is lost

Always searching for the breast

In the center of the garden

We never sit alone

I heard a flower whisper

You're the king of flesh and bone.

Hope

Life is a jewel

It's something to treasure

We move the clouds aside

To make it blue forever

We tell the dreams

To mix with the words

We are the creatures

That sing with the birds.

Eternity of Color

Don't kill the ugly flowers
Let them grow as well
They might be a musty color
But that's not the way they smell
Hold them in the mirror
They might know a spell
They might live forever
While we grow old and frail.

Heaven's Garden

Down the spiral staircase

Following a dove

This garden gets attention

From the gardeners above.

Marigolds

She wears heaven's crown

But she doesn't know it's there

It leaves wavy circles

On the surface of her hair

Maybe it's a halo

If it was she wouldn't care

She sleeps with the marigolds

That over grow the chair.

Love and Spring

I was born in March

By the shady oak

Crawling out of bed

To join the other folk

Names were not important then

All we had was hope

Simple times and dandelions

I just listened as they spoke.

Into The Wood

I have planted flowers
In the ruins of my love
Found a sacred tree
And carved a heart into the wood
Nail my hand to god
Or at least to something good
We have painted saints
On debris from ancient floods.

In My Hand

I create the moment
With a flower in my hand
I make it bright and beautiful
And hard to understand
In my circle of creation
I've formulized a plan
Depicted in the hieroglyphs
Of every Christian man.

Holy Flowers

Holy light
Find the cornerstone
Read the secret words
You'll never be alone
I always wanted love
And what you wanted was unknown
I plant flowers on my soul
to hide the ugly bones.

Collected Time

I've collected flowers
They've collected time
Dust is on their petals
Like lips are onto wine
I could give you heaven
All the planets in a line
Our lives become components
Of an architect's design.

Cemetery Lake

When a flower dies

All the petals break

The stem becomes a corpse

And the colors start to flake

Rain touches the flesh

To take away the ache

The flower is a ghost

In a cemetery lake.

We become the lavender

That blossoms in the end

SIX SECRETS

Beyond the bright lights of the city there is the faint glow of a secret forest. This particular forest is not so different than those you read about in fairy tales. It has many beautiful creatures that lounge about in vast meadows and small insects that leap along lilies, across large bodies of water.

Long ago there was a devastating sadness introduced to the ecosystem of this society that caused the trees surrounding the ancient forest to hold a meeting in secrecy. Their trunks stood like giant pillars of faith, eventually branching together to form a forest temple.

The eldest and most wise creatures of this realm attended the meeting where they were asked to sign a secret pact of utmost importance: to never reveal the secrets of this sacred place to any outsider of the forest.

The sadness itself, seemed small and unimportant, but the old trees of the forest and the Old Rabbit priest felt it was the influence of the outside world that had caused its presence. They felt that it was much more than just a random sadness, it was a well-known disaster that some worried would one day take every breath of life from this enchanted place.

After the meeting, the trees spread apart for miles, pushing the outside world farther and farther away so that not one impure or unworthy creature might find the hidden entrance to this old society, where nature's language is spoken with the symbols of existence, recognized by every living thing.

Many Years Later...

While gathering acorns for the coming winter, a squirrel ventured to the edge of the forest. He stood before the tall arched entrance where he noticed that on one of the eldest of the enormous trees there was something carved into its fading surface, as if hidden by the aged and heavy dusts of time.

The Squirrel asked the honorable looking tree, "What is carved into your chest, my friend?" The Tree replied that it was a heart, it was carved by the Old Rabbit long before the forest was closed off to the outside world.

"A heart?" asked the Squirrel. "Yes, young creature, it is a universal symbol of love." The Squirrel looked at the Tree with amazement because he had just used a concept that was long ago forbidden in the forest, the mysterious concept of love.

The Tree laughed at the Squirrel's silly questions and innocent intentions. The Tree then explained that love is something that requires sacrifice, that all creatures were capable of love before the sadness came and cast its Cimmerian shade over the infrastructure of our lives.

Confused by this, the Squirrel then asked, "Why is the sadness here, Tree, and how long will it last?" The expression on the Tree's face changed from confident and pleasant to a long wooden frown. The Tree explained that the sadness was part of an ancient subversion that now controls the system of this secret place. The Squirrel traced out the heart on the tree's trunk with his paw and the Tree's face stretched back into a generous smile once again. "My dear Squirrel, promise me something before you bed down for the night?" The Squirrel leaned against the Tree, the leaves covering his body like a blanket of crumbling emeralds as he whispered to the tree, "Anything you wish, my friend."

The Tree saw beyond the physical realm, he saw past the winter fur, through the color and sound of the Squirrel's vibration, where he viewed the microcosm of an innocent creature that was begging for the chance to show the world what part he played in the great cycle of the cosmos.

The wise old Tree then said in a loud, commanding voice, "NEVER forget what I have told you about the existence of love." The Squirrel looked up at the Tree with his eyes open wide and his ears large and alert, staying reserved as he listened.

The Tree went on to explain that our world was once a place of rare kindness and incredible brilliance. Its rivers were the veins of this earth and its breath was the voice of the ages. There will always be sadness in our lives, but in that moment of intense longing and regret, remember that love and the belief in a heavenly author is the common thread that holds our worlds together. The Tree then spoke of a time when the Old Rabbit took an oath, where he advised the elders of the provinces of a long awaited prophecy that would forever change the universal beliefs of the forest. He suggested that they prepare and preserve themselves for the coming of this important ethereal shift. The fulfillment of the prophecy would bring new light and knowledge that would be used to extinguish the sadness and drive it into the hollowness of the serpent's belly once and for all.

"Rest, Squirrel, and dream of tomorrow as if it were budding on the branches of today." The Tree closed his eyes and sunk back down into the soil to dwell in the deep root systems of time. "We all have hearts carved into our surface," the Tree said quietly to the Squirrel. "We just haven't realized it yet."

DEO MARTI THINCSO ET DVABVS ALAISAGIS BEDE ET
FIMMILENE ET N AVG GERM CIVES TVIHANTI VSLM

Traveler

I am a traveler

In a field of shining jewels

With a pocket full of raspberries

My heart has broken rules

I've never had a church

Never owned a pair of mules

I built my path to heaven

With another traveler's tools.

This bed has become bothersome.

This Arrow

This arrow is old

Its feathers are stressed

But what it represents

Is holy and clean.

And a success.

Silver Strings

She sleeps with the tulips

She dances for kings

She dug a hole inside my head

To climb into my dreams

Her hands are always dirty

Her face is always clean

I found a secret instrument

With seven silver strings.

Secret Words

I found a lamb
That lived in a well
These secret words
Put the lamb in a spell
The lamb's leg was broken
But love made it well
I gave it my heart
And we climbed out of hell.

Secret Grave

In your lover's room

All your thoughts are safe

But love is not the only secret

Needing to be saved

bodies are forever

When forever is a day

We bury all of heavens horses

In an angel's grave.

Secret Alphabet

If you hold my hand
I'll show you the way
I write down the secrets
Cause the secrets you should save
The alphabet is buried
In Cleopatra's grave
She wrote to the servants
When the pyramids were laid.

Prognosis

The clouds are endless

Evaporating roses

Burn them in candles

And drown them in oceans.

There's a paradox of candles

Waiting for this night

Mostly We Forget

The day is a star

burning out of sight

We multiplied the planets

Times a billion kinds of light

I'll find you a kiss

In the place you'd least expect

A secret place in heaven

That most of us forget.

Melon Patch

I climbed into the melon patch
Look at how they've grown
There I met a hare who said
"You're sitting on my home"
He showed me his palace
And the gold around his throne
We dug our way to hell
But at least we're not alone.

Maritime

My eyes are an ocean

Hazel and blue

The colors of water

That sail me to you

I'll be there soon

God keeps a clock

From mother's canal

Down to the doc.

We think we're important, then we
realize we're all *miniature dolls* under
heaven's unmade bed.

Faith

I fell from the sky

Downward from space

Where sparrows learn to fly

Above the pyramids of faith

I fell from heaven's eye

With a blink upon my face

If you follow me to hell

You might end up back in grace.

Elements

I keep silver flowers
In a crystal bowl
They vibrate my spirit
And it almost moves my soul
If I tell a secret
It's a million whispers old
We make love with angels
That turn secrets into gold.

A Kiss Goodbye

When the day is done

The moon will find the sky

We will read from ancient books

And never wonder why

Children turn to stone

Every flower will be dry

We will dance a eulogy

And kiss the light goodbye.

SEVEN ANGELS

They light up the forest

Like bright eyes in a womb

In Motion

When you find a fallen star
Plant it in the earth

It becomes a flower
In the bedroom of the church

Inside the ball of light
Two angels live inside

Trying to get out
Before our universe collides.

Heaven is an island
Visited by birds
Where angels work for pennies
Splitting planets into thirds.

Rain Angels

I have built a temple
Dedicated pain
And on the altar where I kneel
I wrote an angels name
This has made it simple
For the simple to explain
My love grows inside this rose
And blossoms with the rain.

Many Angels

I walk with angels
Talk with angels
I touch angels
Love angels
I kissed an angel
Angels follow me
I've made angels
Prayed to angels
I have many angels

I'm no angel.

If I'm Wrong

Help me out of here
All my strength is gone
Nail me to a crucifix
And burn me in the lawn
Tell me if I'm right
I'll tell you if you're wrong
In the end my words are whispers
To an angel's song.

My Angel

I have an angel

Lost in the dark

Under the blankets

And over the heart

She speaks in whispers

That crumble apart

When light finds a circle

It dies in the arch.

Carry On

Why do angels cry

Every time they hear a song

The shape of their true nature

Never bends or moves along

They are like the snowflakes

That have gathered on the pond

Thank god they have the strength

To fall and carry on.

Cosmic Love

I went to heaven
It wasn't that far
We held each other
And sat on the car
I met an angel
Who died in a star
She put the planets
Inside of my heart.

Chasing Rain

I am in heaven
I am in pain
I'm making angels
That fold into cranes
I have them dancing
With love on their wings
We're chasing sparrows
And their chasing rain.

Artist

They built a holy temple
To hold the ancient ark
But there's nothing to worship
When the temple falls apart
A thousand broken pieces
Of an angel's broken heart
Sitting on the bodies
Of what some consider art.

The Sadness

When love was banished from the forest it was replaced by something hopeless, a sadness that crawled into the hearts and minds of the creatures. This condition came to be known by all the animals of the forest as, *Beda,* a celestial mechanism that holds limbs into place and moves our bodies into shapes that bend and stretch against our will.

The creatures of this forest are archetypes of love, but in every heart there is a place reserved for sadness. It was written long ago that two lovers were born in the night sky, and their precipitating components trickled down to our forest the knowledge and responsibility of new life and heavenly rewards. These lovers were royal rulers who came from the chief crossing in heaven.

The Old Rabbit left a cipher that would one day be used to remove the final veil that has hung itself upon our forest, so that we may pass through the seven spheres as benevolent creatures. The compassion of these two lovers for the forest and its creatures will re-magnetize the ancient healing mounds.

Love will once again be restored as the primary source of light, and the sadness that has turned our fields and mountains into this funeral pyre of silence will be swallowed whole.

Keep in mind creatures of this forest that in every enchanted place there is an unsolved puzzle, and the key that opens the ziggurat is not always the physical kind.

Soon the sadness will reach full capacity and the prophecy of our forest will bring with its new light a final choice: Will we open our forest to the outside world? Or will we be buried and forgotten in the dark billowing shadows of eternity?

We sail on crescent boats
Through starry skies of precious hope

EIGHT DREAMS

Witness

Bring me the flower

That lives in the winter

Throw out the wicked

Then ask it to enter

Dream of my body

Leaving the earth

Wake up the sleeping

To witness a birth.

Take these working hands

Repair these broken dreams

Build a boat and sail to France

To fish their potent streams.

Somewhere Else

If I had a dream

It would be a holy one

The numbers in my heart

Would add a zero to the sun

I need you to love me

And when our love is done

I will join the universe

Cause that's where love is from.

My Dreams

Follow my dreams
My mystery sleep
Thousands of footsteps
From wandering feet
Find me in heaven
Alone for a week
I sleep with lions
Who eat with the sheep.

Chad Fox

A Whisper

Tonight I found a whisper

It was sleeping at my door

I let it climb into my bed

And there it rested more

It opened up a dream to me

And asked me to explore

I know they're only words

But what else are whispers for.

Catch My Drift

I am drifting wood
Down a gentle stream
There's two people fishing
And they want to catch my dream
If you want my heart
It blossoms in the spring
When I wear a crown of gold
I feel like a king.

My heart is always true

Always full of love

Closer to the human soul

Than pantheons above.

NINE SYMBOLS

HEART

THE HEART ++ A device of love and spirituality. The heart is a universal symbol used and recognized by people around the world.

The Life force – The heart is the life force of the body. The Vital organs are placed around the heart just as the planets are placed around the life giving force of the sun.

Love – Every person has a heart and with it the ability to love and forgive. We are all creatures of compassion and thus the heart is the timeless symbol of love.

"One of the most important points in the elaboration of the role of the heart and of the sphere of tender affectivity is to expose the error of considering them as merely "subjective" or to build up a contrast between "objectivity" and "affectivity.""

Footnotes – The symbol of the heart evolved from the upside-down triangle, which was a symbol of the feminine principle.

CROSS

THE CROSS ++ The meaning behind the cross is a mysterious one. It has been used in almost all religions and yet it is as old as man himself.

The Christian Cross - The death of Christ as symbolized by the cross has been called "the very foundation of the Christian religion" by many scholars.

The Zodiac - There is no doubt that cross is a Christian symbol, but even older than the concept of Christianity is the cross of the Zodiac. The cross breaks a circle down into four equal parts, which become the starting points of the 4 seasons. The mixture of this ancient astrological symbol with the veiled Christian story makes it one of the most widely recognized symbols in the world today.

Footnotes - The term "holy cross" is also known as "heavens cross" which refers to a star constellation that forms a cross.

LADDER

THE LADDER ++ The ladder is one of the most ancient and philosophical symbols on the earth. Its meaning has been symbolically veiled throughout the many cultures and religions of the ancient world.

Jacobs Ladder – The symbolism behind Jacob's ladder of the bible, is one shared by many religions and ancient belief systems, a story of angels that ascend and descend from the heavens.

Genesis 28: 12-13 (KJV) And he [Jacob] dreamed, and behold a ladder set up on the earth, and the top of it reached to heaven: and behold the angels of God ascending and descending on it.

Footnotes – The seven steps to the ladder represent the five planets known to the ancient world and the two luminaries, the sun and moon.

DOVE

COLUMBA THE DOVE ++ Columba was a star constellation in the heavens that took on the attributes of the dove.

The Dove – The ancient peoples called the dove, the dweller of heaven.

Holy Spirit – In the bible Noah releases a dove which brings back to him an olive branch, symbolizing the end of the great flood.

Columbine - c.1310, from M.L. columbina, from L.L. columbina "verbena," fem. of L. columbinus "dovelike," from columba "dove." The inverted flower supposedly resembles a cluster of five doves.

Footnotes – Many legends around the world claim that the devil and his witches can turn themselves into any bird shape accept the dove.

PELICAN

THE PELICAN ++ The pelican is a symbol of self sacrifice. Some of the oldest depictions of the pelican, middle ages, show a pelican piercing its skin to nourish its starving children with its blood.

Jesus Christ – Jesus told his followers "Whoever eats my flesh and drinks my blood has eternal life" making him one of the archetypes of the "Savior."

Pelican - O.E. pellicane, from L.L. pelecanus, from Gk. pelekan "pelican" (so used by Aristotle), apparently related to pelekas "woodpecker" and pelekys "ax," perhaps so called from the shape of the bird's bill.

Footnotes – The father pelican in mythology rips open his own heart to revive his children by drenching them with his life's blood.

OWL

THE OWL ++ The owl is an ancient symbol of wisdom and knowledge.

Owl Protection – Native Americans saw the owl as a protector against evil spirits, giving knowledge only to those who were worthy of accepting it.

The Screech Owl – In the Bible, Adam, names the screeching owl "Lillith" and associates it with a Mesopotamian storm demon.

Book of Isaiah (KJV) - "The wild beasts of the desert shall also meet with the wild beasts of the island, and the satyr shall cry to his fellow; the screech owl also shall rest there, and find for herself a place of rest."

Footnotes – Many cultures have associated these attributes to the owl: intelligence, brilliance, wisdom, power, knowledge.

ACACIA

THE MYSTICAL ACACIA ++ The acacia tree is an umbrella shaped tree that is found in Africa, Australia, and parts of Asia. It produces an edible bean and a fragrant flower.

The Spiritual Acacia – The branch of the acacia tree has been used by people to cast away evil spirits. Some say that it represents the soul and is sometimes used in funerals as a symbol of resurrection.

Acacia - 1540s, from L. acacia, from Gk. akakia "thorny Egyptian tree," probably related to Gk. ake "point, thorn," from PIE base *ak- "sharp" (see acrid). Perhaps a Hellenization of some Egyptian word.

Footnotes – In Egypt the acacia leaves were used as a brush for painting and the flowers were used to make incense for rituals and perfumes.

LAMB

THE LAMB ++ Over the ages the lamb has been associated with many different religious icons, and belief systems.

God's Lamb – The bible, as well as multiple other religious texts, speak of God's son as being the Lamb of God, who becomes the savior of mankind.

The Sign of Aries – In astrology, the sign of Aries is represented by a celestial ram/lamb. Aries is the first of the twelve houses of the Zodiac.

Lamb - O.E. lamb, from P.Gmc. *lambaz (cf. O.N., O.Fris., Goth. lamb, M.H.G. lamp, Ger. lamm "lamb").

Footnotes – In iconography a lamb with a halo and cross is known as an Agnus Dei.

LION

THE LION ++ The lion is an animal of courage and strength. The golden mane of the adult lion represents the long rays of the sun.

Sovereignty – The Lion has been the emblem of many countries, and is the supreme symbol of sovereignty.

The Lioness – Egypt worshiped the lioness as a war deity, known for being brave in battle.

Lion - late 12c., from O.Fr. lion, from L. leonem (nom. leo), from Gk. leon (gen. leontos), from a non-I.E. language, perhaps Semitic (cf. Heb. labi "lion," pl. lebaim; Egyptian labai, lawai "lioness").

Footnotes – In astrology the sign of Leo is symbolized by the solar lion.